MW01442887

The Gradebook
BY KRISTINA CUNNINGHAM

The Gradebook
BY KRISTINA CUNNINGHAM

Dedicated to all of the phenomenal teachers,
thank you for all you do!

Contents

The Project   5

The Girl   24

My Parents   50

Her Parents   58

Gone   65

Away from Him   74

Surprises   86

The Gradebook   94

The Project

Parents are classified into two types, those who care about grades and those who don't. There is no in-between, trust me. From elementary school, where we were graded for coloring inside of the lines, my parents have always been the ones that care about my grades. My mother is always telling me that there is always room for improvement, which I agree with completely. But, having to have a 100 in every class and a 100 on every assignment in every class to me is a bit much.

Now sitting on my bed with my Windows laptop laying on my lap, there are so many numbers illuminating my face. I am looking eye to eye with my mother and father trying not to blink. I have already taken several bathroom breaks and instead said that I forgot my login that I have had for the past ten years and distracted them with the view outside my window. I even started to talk to my small dog, Newton. Don't ask me why that is his name, my parents are really into Calculus for some reason. I did everything in my power to stall, I did not want them to see my 98 in AP Calculus. Last time I checked, a 98 in a class that no other freshman is taking is a pretty darn good grade.

But, tears were already starting to form in my eye glands.

"Nellie?" My mother usually never puts up for fake tears, but I thought I might give it a try. I wiped the fabricated tears away and started to turn my computer in their direction when suddenly there was a sharp ringing sound coming from the front door. My parents both looked in the direction of my bedroom door as if they didn't know where the sound was coming from. I slammed my computer shut and stuffed it into my backpack. I kissed my parents' confused faces goodbye quickly and sprinted out of the door and down the stairs and out the door.

"Nellie Peterson!!" I heard them both roar from upstairs.

I prayed for my butt when I got back in the house that evening, but for now, I was just going to hope they didn't follow me to school.

Right outside the front door stood my best friend in the whole world, Dana. She always had the biggest smile on her face to greet me in the morning. I checked my watch and it read "6:45 am." I give her a nice fistbump and then follow her down our dirt path to her Toyota Corolla Hatchback parked in front of our house.

"How are you doing, Nells?" She was skipping, her car key was jangling on her bright pink key chain. I replied with a subtle nod of my head. She stopped in her tracks, nearly tripping me. I tried to act as if I didn't notice as I hopped into the passenger seat. After a couple of minutes, she finally started the car.

"Grade book day?" Dana mumbled.

"Yep." I pulled my seatbelt on and clicked it into place. Checking that it is fastened correctly, I tug it a few times. I have been friends with Dana for so long that I just know what she is thinking based on her facial expressions.

Her bottom lip was quivering and her eyes were fixed on everything in front of her. Her parents are the type of parents that couldn't care less about her grades. They just want her to do her best in school. Dana is right now probably furious with my parents and worried about my mental health. I think she has gained two more creases on her forehead just from being friends with me. I continue to tell her not to worry about it, but she insists that my parents are evil.

I decided to stop looking at her and instead just look at all of the houses we passed, all of the cars on the road. I could only see numbers circling everything. One house looked to be about 10 feet high, but I would also have to calculate the length and the width of all of the connecting cubes to evaluate the volume. I don't want to be an architectural designer by any means, but numbers are just drilled into my brain. It often hurts my head to even check the time.

My brain often wanders around. I can't help but start thinking about derivatives out of the blue. My AP Calculus teacher taught us that they come in handy when solving problems dealing with rates of change. I like to call these random thoughts my "mind boggles". Currently, I am trying to imagine what that concept would look like written out on paper or right in front of me on the road as cars are speeding down the lanes. Unfortunately, all this does is give me a headache, I close my eyes to relieve some of the pain.

"You have to see a doctor about that, Nellie." I open my eyes and look over at Dana, who is still focused on the road ahead of her. My mouth opens then I close it again. I peer down at my backpack. I have a massive AP Calculus test coming up and I couldn't help but think about studying.

I grab my blue flashcards in my blue folder labeled with the words "AP Calculus". I read out the first card aloud.

"When f '(x) is positive, f(x) is.." I scratch the top of my head in hopes that the answer will come to me. From the corner of my eye, I can see Dana rubbing the bottom of her chin. She is a sophomore in high school and taking Algebra 1 for the second time, so it is strange to me that she is trying to think of something. No offense to her of course, I guess it is nice of her to be helpful.

A light bulb goes off in my head and I come up with the answer.

"Increasing... Yes!!" I look over at Dana to see a surprised look on her face, I lightly chuckle and flip to the next card in the stack. But before I could read the last flashcard, I noticed that we were already in the school parking lot. Either it took me a long time to come up with that answer or Dana was going over the 35-mile-per-hour speed limit.

I hear Dana unbuckle her seatbelt and I decide to do the same. I hit the stack of cards in the palm of my hand to straighten them out into an even stack. I do not have obsessive-compulsive disorder, I think that organization runs in my family. I put the blue cards back into the blue AP Calculus folder.

Dana takes the keys out of the keyhole and looks over at me. I am still holding my folder and I briefly pause to see how impatient she is getting. I can tell that her smile is shrinking by the second, so I hastily throw my blue folder into my backpack and zip it up tight.

At this point, Dana is outside of the vehicle breathing on the glass of her driver-side window.

"Ha ha... I'm coming!" I shoot her with my signature duck face that she only gets to see, it makes her laugh and also buys me some time in situations where her patience is dying. I open the door slowly just to mess with her then I jump out of my seat and close the door behind me.

"You are SO funny Nells, but seriously?" I could sense the concern all over her face because we were almost going to be late for AP Biology, her favorite class. I am not fond of the class because it is split into a group of jocks that are just in the class to meet girls and people that probably don't even know how to spell "Biology". Who am I kidding, those are the same people.

Dana is once again skipping, but this time down the crosswalk leading to the front of the school. I casually walk, trying to rid myself of all stares from the other students walking in, but Dana doesn't seem to have the same plan.

"Hey Dawn, wait up!" I am audibly panting behind her, but she doesn't seem to hear my heart pumping out of my chest. Chess club and study sessions have been my only extracurriculars, which don't tend to work on anything remotely to do with physical exercise. I have PE 1 second block, but I just use it as a study block because khakis and sweat don't mix well. My parents have refused to let me get gym clothes because they believe that I might somehow turn away from my school work and start playing sports.

I can finally see the school doors and I look up in relief. Dana always greets all the staff with a handshake and a nice hello, but I just nod because it is too early in the morning for all of her energy. I keep on thinking that maybe she should cut back on coffee, but I don't want to see her without it.

Our AP Biology class is one of the first doors when we enter the school, which often makes me more confused about why Dana rushes in.

"How are you doing, Petronella Peterson?" I cringe at the sound of my full legal name. I notice that it is Jacoby Briant. I turn my eyes in the other direction and book it into the classroom. I ignore his existence completely.

"Did you see me at the game last night, Petronella?" He falls into the group with the jocks and he is for some reason obsessed with talking to me when I couldn't care less. Dana tells him to stop constantly, but I think it only ignites the fire inside of him. Also, he knows I don't go to football games, but he always asks me random trivia questions about them anyway.

The football boys sit in a huddle around each other, talking about probably something highly outrageous. I form a brilliant comeback in my head when the school bell suddenly rings. The boys all shuffle to their seats slowly to sit down and our teacher, Mrs. Berkeley, starts to type up something on her keyboard.

Everything she types appears on the fairly large screen attached to the wall at the front of the classroom:

```
Groups for Biomolecules Project:
```

I start to read what she is writing on the board and then panic. I despise group projects, especially in this class. I usually just work with Dana when I can, but in this situation, it seemed as though Mrs. Berkeley would be selecting the teams. I look down at her fingers as they are typing, I have memorized the position of all of the letters on the keyboard so I refrain from looking at the board. She types "J" and then pauses to look up at us again, rubbing the bottom of her chin. She types "A", then "C", then "I", and erases the "I" quickly as though we didn't notice her mistake. As time passes, I look up at the screen because I lose track of all of the letters:

JACOBY AND CALEB

NELLIE AND DANA

I let out all of the air I am holding in and smile at Dana who is sitting right behind me. She smiles back and gives me a celebratory high-five. That is just when I see a hand go up in my peripheral vision. It seems to be Jacoby, I predict it is probably just another silly comment about something random.

"Caleb is not going to be here all week and Nellie always works with Dana, mam." I let out an apparent groan and I can hear Dana do the same. I don't know why I didn't notice that earlier and why Jacoby has to always mess with Mrs. Berkeley's plans.

Mrs. Berkeley nods her head and pops out her bottom lip in agreement with Jacoby's proposition. I look down at my desk and shake my head aggressively in disagreement with his proposition. She notices and chuckles softly.

"Nellie, it is always good to meet new people." She explained to me.

But what she didn't know is I already met him and I made up my decision that I was never going to join up with him. I groan again but louder and look up at the board to see the most horrific sight:

```
JACOBY AND NELLIE
```

I peer over at Jacoby and he is giving fistbumps to all of the boys next to him and they have ludicrous smirks on their faces. Jacoby has never been one to care about his grades. He has mentioned multiple times that he didn't know we had grades. I knew he was joking but his parents' standards of grades must not be as high as mine are.

The two things Jacoby ever talks about are football and more football, I was not fond of the sport and did not intend on hearing about it. As soon as all of the groups were assigned, everyone just stared at each other awkwardly. Dana got to work with a female, so I wouldn't say that she is complaining as much as I am.

Jacoby rushes over to my desk with the biggest smile on his face. I give him a fabricated smile in return, just to get this experience over with faster. He sits at the desk next to me and puts on his typical confused face. I look up at the board again to see a word written next to our names.

"I guess we're doing our project on Carbohydrates." I look back at Jacoby and he is still lost for words.

"Have you ever had a banana or bread for that matter?" I hope he remembers what Carbs are because we just learned about them yesterday, one day ago.

I snap in his face to get him to respond, but he is just staring at me. I can't imagine what he is possibly thinking of. My face goes red as time goes ticking down in this class period. I finally just gave up trying to read his mind.

"Jacoby, what is it?"

"Why don't you like me?" He replied in a subtle tone.

My whole face changed shades of red. I started fidgeting with my fingers under my desk and couldn't help but quietly tap my foot on the floor a lot. I looked back at the board to divert my eyes from the situation occurring at hand. I look around the classroom as well to catch any staring eyes.

"Why don't you like me, Nellie?" He questioned again, but like ten octaves lower than the first.

I open my mouth then close it again then open it again over and over. I probably look like Pac-Man in real life right now. I need to think this question through and he has just put me on a shot clock, not that I watch the basketball games either.

The bell rings to mark the end of the first block. I look over at his face and it looks colder than usual. There are single spots of red illuminating the sides of his face. I grab my backpack from behind my desk and walk out the door.

I walk quicker than I typically do to PE because I know Jacoby has the same class 2nd block and if he catches me in the hallway, there is no escape. I feel a light tap on my shoulder and my heart skips a beat.

"Nells, how did it go with Jacoby?" I was relieved that it was Dana. I slow down so we can walk next to each other. I give her a slight giggle as to draw her off the scent of the conversation I had with him... or I guess the question he asked me. She giggled as I hoped and then she started speed walking.

She doesn't have PE next so I have no barrier between myself and Jacoby with his random remarks. I am not prepared to see him face to face again because I fear what he will ask me next.

"Bye, Nellie, see you after!" I wave goodbye to Dana as she slides into her drawing class and I continue walking down the long hallway. I hear Jacoby's voice creeping behind me, so I run into the nearest bathroom to hide. Only did I know it wasn't a girl's bathroom, so after seeing a glimpse of a young man walking in, I stood outside of the bathroom listening for Jacoby's voice. It was very unique and nobody could miss it.

Once it finally faded away, I stepped back into the hallway and started walking toward the gym. We only had seven minutes to get to class and I didn't want to be marked tardy. I eventually see the two large swinging wooden doors leading into the gym. I look left and right to see if Jacoby is around, he is nowhere in sight so I walk through.

I go to the furthest bleachers away from the entrance of the gym and I lug all my backpack up the ten steps to eventually sit at the very top. I am panting again, so I sit down quickly and grab my water bottle tucked inside the pocket on the side of my backpack. I press the bottom on the side of the water bottle and the lid opens quickly. I have a few sips of the ice-cold water then I return the water bottle to its designated pocket.

I look up and scan the gym from the left to the right. I see a group of girls and boys playing a game of "Knockout" at the basketball hoop. Even Leonard was playing, one of the people in my AP Calculus class next block who always sits down during PE right beside me. We usually test each other during the second half of the class, but it seems like he has other plans. So, I reach into my backpack to find the blue folder again holding the blue flashcards.

I flipped through the first few because they were fairly easy. I come up on one that is tricky so I just stare at it for a few minutes. I suddenly feel a great vibration coming from the bottom of the bleachers. I peek behind my flashcards and it is Jacoby coming up the steps toward me. I look directly down at my shoes.

"Nellie, what happened back there?" He must have noticed that I was sitting up here when he arrived and he seems to be keen to get an answer to his question. I didn't know how to answer it, I thought it was pretty obvious why I didn't like him. He was always calling me out in every class and was the only one that made fun of my full name and used it for that matter.

I look up at his face right in front of me. He is standing three inches in front of me and looking into my eyes. I instinctively look back down again but now at my flashcards again. I try to look bothered to possibly get him to leave me alone and go back to throwing a football around with his friends. He snatches the stack of cards I am looking at out of my hands. I grunt loudly to get his attention.

"-sin(x)? Tricky one, huh..." He intensely analyzes the card in the palms of his hands.

"Jacoby, please give them back, I have a massive AP Calc test next block!" I put my right hand out so he can place them right into my hands.

"D over d times x all multiplied by cos sign." He flips over the card and sees that he is correct. I was beyond surprised, he was currently taking Algebra 1 with Dana. He has never shown any amount of intelligence before. I grew more skeptical by the second.

"Jacoby, why do you take Algebra 1 if you know Calculus?"

He looked up at the ceiling as if he was forming an answer in his head. He eventually looked back down at me and looked me in the eyes again.

"I like learning, but if the football guys know that, they would probably clown me." He answered.

My eyes shot open. He liked to learn. That was interesting, I always figured that since his parents didn't care about his grades, they didn't care about learning either. But my hypothesis seems to be proven incorrect. I nod my head so he knows I heard him and he hands me my cards back.

"I came over here to possibly work on our project if you want to?"

I put my blues cards back into my blue folder, then I put it all away into my backpack. I found a clipboard in my backpack with a few sheets of lined paper attached to it. I pull it out and dig around to find a pencil with a sharp tip. I pat the seat next to me to signal Jacoby to sit down. He follows my instructions then I start to feel his hot breath on my neck.

"Okay, so Carbohydrates." I move over slightly and put the clipboard and pencil in between both of us. He starts to write something on the top paper:

Carbohydrates - Sugar molecules, the body breaks down into glucose.

I was surprised again as it looked like he knew about biomolecules too. I guess the jocks weren't just trying to meet girls, some of them were actually studious. I lifted the clipboard off of the bleachers and took the pencil with it. I started to draw the Carbohydrate structure right below his writing.

"Nellie, why don't you like me?" He asks the question again and I freeze in place. I put the pencil back on the clipboard and looked back up at him.

"I didn't like you because I thought that you didn't like me." I finally reveal the truth then I quickly look back down so I don't catch his reaction to my answer.

The Girl

I am just staring at the food on my plate in front of me. There are three boiled eggs on my plate all laying on a slice of toast. Steam is rising into the air off of my breakfast. I decide to instead take a sip of the milk sitting behind my plate.

I pass the plate and pass the milk to see football being played on the television. I usually always watch reruns of our school football team's games after a big home game. We played against a school with the mascot of Jaguars last night and it was a pretty tough game, but we won 20 to 17. I'm the quarterback of the team and it was a lot of pressure on me to call the play, I was sweating from head to toe and could only see the massive crowd in all ten stands.

My parents both leave for work around 4 am to go to their bakery, so I typically just get ready until 6 am. We have football practice and game review at 6:15 am every morning, so I get to school relatively early. If anyone misses the morning, we all have to do sprints down the field or up and down the stairs in the school if it is raining. I don't mind doing sprints, but I try to always make it on time so I am not tackled by everyone else on the team.

I am watching the fourth quarter where the game turned around. The camera zooms up on me, I am holding the football directly looking at Liam, number 23. I catch the other team off guard by throwing a forward pass in the complete other direction to Peet on the field.

Suddenly, a sharp ringing noise erupts from my phone and I run up to the television to turn it off. We always tap all of our remotes on the wall next to each television so we never lose any of the remotes. I turn off the alarm on my phone which is letting me know it is 6 am.

I grab all my bags at the front door and head out to my car. I own a Bentley Bacalar that my grandparents bought for me for my last birthday. My parents refused to take any of their money because they believe that they can accumulate it on their own. And they own a very successful bakery company, but nowhere near my grandparents' technology company. They make around 40 million together per year and since I am their only grandchild, they intend on spoiling me and I won't complain.

I turn around and do a quick back peddle to the driver's seat. I am constantly working on my calves because a few years ago I had to get calf surgery and it weakened my lower body altogether. My parents were terrified and almost didn't let me get back into football, but I convinced them that this is what I wanted to do for a living.

I finally reached the door after a few seconds. I press the open button on my keys and throw all of my stuff on the passenger seat. I jump into my seat and shift to drive. I slowly take my foot off the gas and then start cruising on the road. My roof is off so my shaggy brown hair blows in the wind.

I am now just looking ahead at the black car in front of me. We are both stopped at a red light. My phone starts buzzing in my right pocket. I quickly grab it looks like I missed a call from my mom from five minutes ago that I probably just missed. A voicemail notification pops up and I click on it after my face opens my phone. An aggressive honk comes from behind my car and I look ahead to see that the light is now green.

I press on the gas and start driving again, I look into my rearview mirror to see the driver behind me mouthing the word "finally". He even throws his arms up as if he just lost 200 dollars because he bet on the Tampa Bay Buccaneers. No hate against them, they're just the worst NFL team statistically.

The voicemail message starts playing after a few seconds.

"Jacoby, I know you are heading to school now, but I wanted to let you know that your dad and I have to work late at the bakery tonight for the big sale. We will talk to you late tonight, love you!"

I am not a huge fan of the job my parents have, they are constantly leaving for something with the bakery and I never really see them anymore. Starting high school has just made it worse because now I can drive myself to school and I miss the chats we used to have in the car together. They are just glad that I can drive to school so they can extend their bakery's hours. I continue to tell them that I would like to spend a little more time with them, but they're too busy. They don't even know that I am failing all of my classes besides PE. They couldn't care less about how I am doing.

"Siri, send Mom a thumbs-up emoji!" The least I can do is keep my head up and try to take care of myself. I don't want them to worry about me because they already put enough on my plate. If she thinks I'm okay, then they will both be happy.

I see the next turn coming up and it is the entrance to the school. I make sure there's no car driving straight forward, then I hastily turn to the left. Liam is walking to the school holding his football bag on the front of his body and his school backpack on the back. I feel slightly sorry for him so I pull over and ask if he wants a ride to the weight room. He accepts my offer and pushes my bags onto the floor so he can sit in the passenger seat.

We both head to the weight room parking lot and hop in my car. I look down at my watch and it reads "6:13 am". We both sprint into the gray door that is slightly ajar. Our head coach looks at us with a very confused look on his face as we nearly shove two boys standing behind the door.

"Okay, so I think that is everyone" He announces and we all sigh in relief because our practice in the morning may be cut short.

We start each morning's practice slash review session to praise certain people on the team.

"Jacoby Briant, let's give him a round of applause, awesome work last night!" I try my best not to smile because I didn't want to seem desperate for the praise. Everyone claps quietly and the head coach puts on his reading glasses to read out the remaining names on his sheet of paper. I scream on the inside because I finally did something right.

Due to my injury a few years ago, I have only been able to watch football instead of play, so my game has diminished to none, and for the past weeks, I have had to train myself from the start. This is my first time being acknowledged for something and it feels incredible. I can't wait to tell my parents tonight when they get home.

The head coach reads aloud some other names, but I tune them out because I see that the door is still open.

I peer through the crack to see the student parking lot in the distance. I squint my eyes and see students getting out of their cars to stand in front of the school. I often wonder why someone would want to come to school early, but I try not to judge others for their interesting choices.

"Ok guys, we are going to skip our review for this morning and jump straight into weight training. Pick your equipment and get to work!" Our coach has a very raspy voice and I can rarely pick up what he is saying, but he hand gestures everything so I have just learned to understand that instead.

I decided to follow Liam to the Machine Flys. I've been meaning to work on my chest for a while now because I often forget about it. Our coach is relatively easygoing (probably more than he should be). So, he doesn't give us goals or specific instructions when we have morning weight training.

He wants us to be self-disciplined and also be more organized, but I just think he doesn't care, but I can't assume. It is strange only because one of our players named Johnny always eats his breakfast during weight training instead of working out and our coach doesn't say anything about it.

He is slicing through a stack of pancakes right now after he spent the last five minutes looking for his bottle of syrup in his gym bag. I know I said I don't judge, but I honestly don't know how he made it on the varsity football team. Then again, he is the coach's son so that may have played a part in his decisions during tryouts this year.

I finish my 20th rep on the machine then I stand up to take a break. I currently put on 192 pounds and I am a pretty small guy, so I can't do too many reps yet. I grab my jug of water to take a small sip.

I peer through the opening of the door again and notice a new car is in the parking lot. It seems to be Dana's vehicle because it is covered in white and Dana is also standing right outside of the vehicle, it looks like she is right up on the glass.

I look down at my watch and it is already 7, school is about to begin in fifteen minutes. I must have fallen asleep on the machine or time just flies extremely quickly.

Dana always drives Nellie to school. Nellie seems to despise me for some reason, I always just try to talk to her and she turns in the other direction. I love her first name, Petronella and I don't know why she doesn't go by it. My great-grandmother's name was Petronella and Nellie reminds me so much of her. I only got to see her once and I miss her so much.

Dana always tries to tell me to stop whenever I just want to talk to her, it might just be because I'm a guy on the football team. I wish that she would give me a chance because she is so smart and I love the clear glasses that she always wears and her bright blue eyes.

I wait for Nellie to poke her head out of the car and then I admire her cute long curly blonde hair tied up into a ponytail. I've always wondered what her hair would look like if it was not in a ponytail, but she seems keen on keeping it that way for a long time.

Now I am guzzling water to not make it seem obvious that I am staring at her because the guys often pick on me for having a crush on her. They don't find her attractive in any way, but I like a girl's inside more than her outside. In my opinion, I feel Nellie has an impeccable inside and outside, but I don't want to call attention to myself.

"Jacoby, class starts in a few, you comin'?" I spin around to see Liam right behind me. I noticed that the weight room was now vacant and we were the only two people still in the room.

"Yeah dude, be in class in a sec." I screw my water jug shut and stuff it into my gym bag. I don't ever drink cold water because it always drips everywhere. Most if not everyone in the school knows I'm the football team quarterback, but I don't like the look of carrying around a big jug of water and I also don't like carrying around a massive jug of water.

We have lockers to put our stuff in, but it has always been easier for me to carry my football bag and school bag together. The locker room is so far away from the field and also there is a bathroom to change in right at the field. The other boys only use the locker room because they like to goof around before practice starts in the afternoon.

I went down the hallway and turned left to enter the Academic wing of the school which is right next to the front of the school. I catch a glimpse of Nellie and I speed walk up to her with her back turned. I don't know what to say, so I just try to be polite and also interested in her.

"How are you doing, Petronella Peterson?" I think that saying her full name might get her attention and she might look in my direction so we can finally talk.

I look as though she has been shocked and she turns around to meet me face to face. I open my mouth to say something else but then she pretty much runs into the classroom, almost like she didn't just see me. Dana is next to her and Dana makes a slicing neck motion to tell me to cut it out, but I honestly don't know what I did wrong. I thought I was being nice since I was concerned, no one else seemed to say that, not even the teacher.

I asked her if she would go to the football game yesterday and I think I saw someone who resembled her in the stands last night. I head over to my seat and turn in her direction. The football boys are now crowding around me trying to get my attention. I just stare at Nellie instead and it seems they notice when they start giggling like I can't hear them.

I think up another question, hoping I get some sort of response out of her. "Did you see me at the game last night, Petronella?" I was hoping that she was there and it wasn't just someone who looked like her or that would be pretty embarrassing. I see that she continues to look down at her desk and doesn't pay any attention to me.

"Dude, give it up already. She is not in love with you." Johnny states even combining that remark with some kissy faces which I continue to tell them to stop doing. I so badly want to tell him that he is only on the football team because of his dad, but football is the only thing going for me right now and I don't want to get kicked off the team.

I instead just ignore him and take off my bags to place them beside my desk. The bell rings and they all slowly move to their assigned seats far away from me. Well, except for Liam, but I can stand him more than the other guys.

I notice that Nellie is staring at Mrs. Berkeley and I do the same. She always types on her computer what she could write on the board, but she says her handwriting is atrocious. I have yet to see it, but it couldn't be any worse than mine.

She mentioned yesterday that we were going to be working on a project of our choice to do with the Biomolecules we have been learning about. I love when she picks our groups because then it gets me closer to working with Nellie and she would have no choice but to talk to me. An assertive approach, but not all the fish are going to reel in at the same speed I guess. I have been reeling for 4 months now and she has yet to bite. I am the quarterback on the football team and I don't look ugly, how much more bait does she need?

I read the board and I am with Caleb and Nellie is with Dana for the hundredth time. I feel like she always puts them together for her benefit because they always work perfectly together and get unbelievably high grades.

I looked around the room for Caleb and I remembered he told Mrs. Berkeley he was not going to be here all week because he will be in the hospital. I don't know what for, but if it gets me closer to Nellie, I couldn't care less. I promise I didn't do anything to him... I think I didn't at least.

I come up with a brilliant plan to form the perfect team with Nellie and I raise my hand in hopes that Mrs. Berkeley will agree with my proposition and allow us to work together. She looks at me and points in my direction, but I can also see the petrified face of Nellie in my peripheral vision.

"Caleb is not going to be here all week and Nellie always works with Dana, mam." I usually never say "mam", but I thought I would throw it in there just as the cherry on top. I hear both Nellie and Dana groan, I try to ignore it but it is so apparent and extremely loud. I often wonder why Mrs. Berkeley allows such behavior.

I look back at Mrs. Berkeley to hear her response and she responds with a nod of her head. She backspaces until all of the names are going on the board except for my own. I watch her place Nellie's name next to mine and I am now ecstatic. I look over at Nellie and she is just shaking her head right to left countless times. I think it is pretty cute how her little ponytail has a mind of its own and sticks straight up in the air, waving at Dana behind her.

Mrs. Berkeley thinks it is hilarious and says, "Nellie, it is always good to meet new people." I agree, I'm glad Mrs. Berkeley doesn't know about Nellie's unreasonable beef with me or she would likely take Nellie's side in this situation.

Liam puts his fist out and I give him a fistbump. I don't know what that was for though, this was just step one and I thought all of the football boys thought it was funny. I guess Liam is just the only supportive one. I think that it is funny and we both chuckle. Mission one accomplished! She is now on my hook.

Mrs. Berkeley finished assigning all the groups and my heart was pumping out of my chest because I was actually about to have a conversation with Nellie for the first time, like. This was insane and I didn't want to ruin it. Before she could escape the classroom, I made sure to run over to her desk dodging all the desks like they are people like we do in football.

Once I sit down in the chair next to her, I lose all train of thought. I can't help but just stare into her eyes, I have never been this close to them. They shine as the fluorescent lights in the room bounce off of them. She is so beautiful and I cannot believe I am about to work on a big project with her.

Instead of staring back at me, she looks at the board to see our assigned Biomolecule, there are lipids, carbohydrates, proteins, and nucleic acids.

"I guess we're doing our project on Carbohydrates," she mentions. I honestly cannot even take my eyes off her, I feel myself getting warmer by the second as well. She says something else as well, but I can't seem to hear anything.

She brings her hand up to my face and snaps, causing me to flinch but not move an inch. She looks pretty angry, but this is my one moment to talk to her, I need to say the right thing. I think long and hard for a couple of minutes or many a couple of hours, I lost track of the time. I was lost in her eyes.

Eventually, it seemed like she had enough of me and asked, "Jacoby, what is it?"

I inhale and exhale, then reply with, "Why don't you like me?"

I don't know why I said that. Dumb Jacoby. I had one chance and I messed it up. I guess I would like to know the answer, but I didn't mean to say that out loud, I was supposed to only say that in my head.

Her face turned bright red in response to my awful question. I noticed that she was getting nervous and I noticed all of the signs. Her fingers were playing with each other and her foot was going crazy on the floor, it was like she was playing a Metallica song.

My mouth and my brain must not be connected because I, for some reason, asked the same question again. She was moving her mouth at a rapid pace as if she was going to say something but then she didn't, but then she wanted to say something, but she didn't. I don't know why everything is fighting against me, my life is just crumbling down now.

I was so thankful that at that moment the bell rang. Nellie couldn't have gotten up quicker and sprinted out the door.

Liam was sitting adjacent to me and he saw the entire thing play out. I walk back to my seat to grab my bags, then I head out the door with the group of football boys.

They all start talking about a football game from forever ago and I can't help but continue just looking down at my shoes while I am walking. I can't believe I embarrassed myself again in front of Nellie. One of the guys asks me how it went with my "girlfriend".

I fake laugh and try to come up with a response that won't get me tackled on the field this afternoon.

"It went well, thank you!" Maybe the "thank you" part was too much, this day is just going downhill quickly.

I try to peer over the crowd to see where Nellie could be. I see a glimpse of her backpack running straight into the boy's restroom. Some guy must have the same backpack as Nellie or Nellie just got majorly confused.

I decided to just meet her in PE class to discuss what was going through my head and possibly start working on the project we need to have done in a few days. I see the double doors leading into the gym, I speed walk to get a football first.

We're allowed to throw the football in the gym to one another, but there are only two so I always rush in to grab one before they are both gone because I am only good at football. If I picked up a basketball or attempted to kick a soccer ball, I would probably have to leave the school and the state for that matter.

And before anyone says it, in football, we may kick the ball, but they are two entirely different shapes of balls. I see the football sitting on top of the pile of other balls, it is like a pot of gold on top of all of the other junk replicating a scene in most treasure hunt movies. Really the main character is always only looking for one particular thing, then leaves with the chance of possibly being buried in sand or something like that.

I run to the football and then I see a small girl running from the other direction. I want to be respectful to all females, but I am the quarterback of the football team. I would lose my dignity and spot on the team if I got tackled by Brittany from Algebra 1 class.

Brittany grabs the ball, I jump on her and tackle her for the ball. She starts crying like she usually does all the time. I should have honestly seen it coming. She yells at me to let go of her, but I eventually take the ball away from her and hold it up for all of the football boys to see. They all applaud me. But, out of the corner of my eye, Coach Stickle is walking in my direction.

"Jacoby, quarterback of the football team, nice side tackle!" He claps lightly while looking up at the ball in my hand and then back down at my face. I was in shock, I thought I was for sure going to be going to the principal's office for this one.

"Coach?!" I exclaim.

"No, sit on the bleachers or I'm calling home. And give her back the football." He said in an extremely stern voice.

My parents weren't home and they probably wouldn't care, but I tossed the ball over to her anyway and she dropped it as soon as it landed in her hands. I don't even know why she wanted the ball, she had so much trouble holding it. I see the football boys all moan and then run over to the game of "Knockout" that was happening at the other end of the gym.

I decided to just try to find Nellie amongst all of the students sitting on the bleachers. She always sat in a new seat, likely to avoid me. But, the gym wasn't extremely large, so I could easily spot her sitting at the farthest bleacher, all the way at the top.

I ran all the way and tried to avoid contact with the coach since it seemed like he was not the proudest of me right now.

I tried to climb up the steps quietly, but she still noticed me coming to talk to her. She kept her head down and didn't look back up at me. I didn't know what to say so I just stuck to the conversation my mouth apparently wanted me to have for some reason.

"Nellie, what happened back there?" I questioned. I was just letting my mouth take the lead at this point because it couldn't get any worse than it is now.

She finally looks up at me and I am relieved that she is finally not going to give me the silent treatment. But, then she looks right back down. I notice she is reading off of these blue flashcards. I also notice there is a folder labeled with "AP Calculus" on it. I was very fond of Calculus, I always study it in my free time since I don't have it as a class.

I am scared of what the football team will think if I am in a class filled with a bunch of nerds, in the nicest way possible of course. Nellie is in that class as well. She seems to be just staring at the card, she is probably confused.

I take the cards gently from out of her hands so I can get a better look at the one she is struggling with. I don't even pay attention to her face because I know she is furious at the moment and we are not in a good place with our relationship. I think she is slowly falling off my hook before I have even started reeling her in. She grunts in my face and I ignore the noise.

"-sin(x)? Tricky one huh..." It wasn't tricky at all, I didn't want her to think that I was any smarter than her. She is one of the smartest people I know, yet she doesn't have much competition amongst my football friends.

"Jacoby, please give them back, I have a massive AP Calc test next block!" She informs me. I already knew she had a test, she has been studying for the past month (it feels like) and I intended on giving her a break.

I close my eyes and imagine what the answer would look like in my mind. "D over d times x all multiplied by cos sign." I flipped over the card and it was correct. Her eyebrows perked up and her eyes practically shot out of her head.

"Jacoby, why do you take Algebra 1 if you know Calculus." I tried to think of an intelligent answer, instead, I think I should just tell her the honest answer.

"I like learning, but if the football guys know that, they would probably clown me," I answered.

She made the same face she did 20 seconds ago when she figured out I might be a tad bit smart. She nods because she finally understands. I hand her back her cards so I don't get in trouble again today. I decided that I should probably tell her why I am up here with her.

"I came over here to possibly work on our project if you want to?"

I don't know whether she heard me or not because she is putting away all of the stuff that she had out and getting out a clipboard filled with paper along with a pencil. So either she is about to write a whole bunch of formulas and equations or I don't know what else she would do with that paper.

She invites me to sit next to her and I will never pass up that opportunity. I sit right next to her and look over her shoulder at the blank pieces of paper on the clipboard.

"Okay, so Carbohydrates." She reminds me. I know quite a few things about carbohydrates from being an athlete and just enjoying learning about new things. I watch her push the clipboard in between us and she slides away from me. I pick up her pencil and start writing a few words I can recall about Carbohydrates.

Whenever I look at her now, she looks extremely surprised. It is like she believes all jocks have to be stupid to be jocks. She saw what I had written and she took the clipboard to draw a Carbohydrate structure below it.

I was genuinely curious this time and asked again, "Nellie, why don't you like me?" She seemed to like my company, yet every other time when we are not working on school work, she always shuts me off from communicating with her. I don't know what I did to make her feel this way.

She finally replied for the first time, "I didn't like you because I thought that you didn't like me." I hear the truth and I am kind of surprised. Why would she care about how I felt about her? She even had her head down so I could look into her eyes.

"I do like you, Nellie. I don't know what I did to make you not like me. You always hate when I talk to you." She finally looks up at me when I reply. Her face is flooded with tears.

"Jacoby, I didn't think anyone liked me. My own parents don't like me unless I get a freaking 100 on everything. I just expected that from everyone now."

I wrap one of my arms around her and she puts both of her arms around me. I didn't know this was just about grades. If her parents saw my grades they would likely kick me out of their house. I guess I didn't take into account how much her grades have meant to her. I don't recall her ever having below 100 in any of our classes.

"Well, I have to go to AP Calculus before the bell rings." She wipes the tears quickly from her face then she packs up all of her stuff.

"Nellie, are you sure you are okay?" I am actually concerned for her mental health right now. I look down at all of the students rushing out of the gym doors. After checking my watch, I realize that we only have 3 more minutes to get to class.

Time went extremely fast and I was not prepared for what was going to come from that conversation. It felt like she was holding that in forever. I think I am the first person she has told that to, I try to hold back tears of my own. My face turns a definite shade of red though.

The football boys are already gone, but I wouldn't want to be known as the quarterback that cries and likes smart girls that are unattractive in their made-up book.

My Parents

I sprint down the school hallway because I am almost late to my AP Calculus and I didn't even get to study through PE because of Jacoby. I guess he is smarter and more sweet than I thought.

I can't help but replay the moment in my head a million times over again. It was so embarrassing. I went from not even talking to him to crying on his shoulder and he let me. I guess he is not so bad, but if I fail this AP Calculus test because I was talking to him when I could have been studying, my parents will go off.

I have never failed any test in my life or any assignment. "Failed" in my parent's book means a 99 or below.

I still have the 98 in this class that they don't know about and I don't intend them to know about. Our AP Calculus teacher always grades our test on a scantron and as long as I finish before the second half of class, she will have the grades in before I leave, thus changing my grade from a 98 to a 100.

The tests are always extremely lengthy though and we only get an hour to finish them. I usually finish at the 30-minute mark, but since the only thing flooding my brain is Jacoby, I cannot focus.

I arrive in the classroom with a few seconds to spare and the manilla folders are standing on each of our desks. My heart started to beat a little faster and it was already going pretty fast since I ran to this class. Our teacher, Mr. Olive notices that everyone is in the classroom and he opens his file cabinet with the small silver key that he keeps tied to his ID on his keychain.

Inside the file cabinet, he pulls several sheets of paper. He divides them into two stacks that seem to be two different types of paper. One being the bubbles to fill in and the other being the test that we are never allowed to write on because he uses it for all of his other classes.

He explains that exact thing aloud to the class even though we have heard the lecture around 20 times now. After he is finished speaking and answering unneeded questions that are just running down our time, I receive a thick test packet and the bubbles or scantron to go along with it.

I shake my pencil back and forth. My feet both tap rapidly now and sweat comes rushing down my face.

I don't at all feel prepared for the test anymore, I feel like I have forgotten pretty much everything. I can only think about Jacoby, I have placed my problem and worry on him and he is likely crumbling under the pressure as well now.

There is always a lined piece of paper on each of our desks as well to do our figuring on. I read the first few questions to get a grasp of the difficulty of this test. I breathe in and out, then fill in the first bubble.

I am feeling a little more confident now and my pace has increased. I know that I have gotten all of them right so far. I continue on the test, almost halfway through now and only 15 minutes have passed so I am in a good time. I briefly look around me and everyone else is sweating as much as me, it stinks of BO and loaded grandpa cologne in this classroom.

Every few seconds someone asks to leave for the restroom and just doesn't come back. You would think that Mr. Olive would catch on, but he is too busy probably reading emails or playing Tetris on his computer.

Those students are likely crying or calling their mom to pick them up from school early because they "vomited" in the bathroom toilet. Someone did vomit one time, but everyone has just been stealing her story ever since to get an additional day to take the test. Mr. Olive just uses a different format of the test and they have to stay after school one day to finish it.

Our class average at the moment is 68 and for some reason, no one sees a problem there. Half of the class has dropped and the other half has complained to the principal about the level of difficulty in the class. Don't get me wrong, Mr. Olive is a great teacher, but some people don't absorb information as quickly as I do.

I am finally finished with the test and I hand it in to Mr. Olive to scan. He pulls out his phone and presses a few buttons before he scans the test. His face changes rapidly to one that looks extremely confused.

My heart starts beating like crazy.

"Is something wrong, sir?" I ask in a gentle tone. He presses a button on his phone again and scans my test again.

"You got a 99, great job!" I grow cold and my sight starts to get increasingly blurry, my legs are so straight and tight. My heart feels like it just dropped. One second I am in the classroom, the next second, I am laying in my bedroom at home and two blurry blobs were in the shape of my parents.

"Nellie, do you want to explain this to us?" I didn't know whether she was talking about the horrible grade I got on the test or the fact that I passed out on the ground in front of my entire AP Calculus class.

She was holding up my scantron paper with a red "99" on it. I don't know whether to be upset that my mother doesn't care that I could have seriously been injured or the audacity that Mr. Olive had to see that I was passed out and still write my grade on the scantron to give to my parents.

"No TV, no computer, no phone, no time outside of the house besides school, Dana's parents know this too. You will only have your bed in here and that is even a privilege." My mother had her mouth moving around 75 miles per minute. I was still trying to correct my vision so I could see her clearly and she was more worried about the 99 I had in AP Calculus now.

"Yes, mam." Or at least I thought that was my mom who was speaking. I felt like I was in a nightmare, my worst nightmare had finally come true.

My mom had that face like she felt like she just did something amazing. She did not, and she just crushed her daughter who is trying her best for her, but she is never going to be proud of me it feels like.
    I watch as my dad takes out all of my belongings and carries them into the room next to me. My mom was too frustrated to even look at me anymore and she made him do it all himself.

My dad is not as strict as my mom, but he does go along with the rules that she has put in place, which makes him just as strict in my opinion. He is breathing extremely heavily as he carries the dresser out of my room and he has COPD as well, so it makes my mom that much more insensitive. I would help him, but he is currently taking out all of my stuff, so I quickly change my mind.

After a few short minutes because I didn't own that many things to begin with and my dad was rushing to get the job done so he could rest.

I am just here sitting on my bed, staring at the wall in front of me. I can still only think of Jacoby. I wonder how he is doing. I hate to say it, but I may have a crush on him. All those times when I just told him to leave me alone, I could have been growing closer with him and he could have comforted me through all of this headache.

When I was sitting on those bleachers right beside him, my heart felt warm and I felt safe talking to him about my parents.

I get up to open my window, so I can at least look at something besides painted walls. I prop my pillows up at the top of my bed straight up in the air and I sit up on them. Once I hear their bedroom door close and squeak loudly as it did, I realize that my parents probably went back to sleep, they are both ER nurses, so they typically only work during the evening until the early morning and just sleep during the day.

I finally feel it hit me. I have just failed. I am a failure. Everything I have done up until now has meant nothing. According to my parents, anything below 100 is not perfect. So I guess I'm just dumb now.

Tears come streaming down my face and I now understand what it is like to not get a 100. My parents told me they have never gotten anything other than 100 in all of their classes and I have finally broken that cycle. I know they are very disappointed in me and I should be very disappointed in myself.

But, talking to Jacoby was so soothing and it was the best moment of my life. I did not think that was ever going to be the best moment of my life. I would give all my money away to talk to him again. I've already poured out so much into him and I just want his company.

Her Parents

I walk into my house around 3 in the afternoon because our head football coach cancels practice. It was only lightly drizzling, but he seemed to know best. My back was killing me after I lugged all of my football stuff all around the school today.

We have a couple of hooks behind our front door, so I put my stuff up there. I close the door behind me to find Nellie behind the door, she is soaking wet from head to toe and seems to be shivering as well. I scream uncontrollably and she jumps.

"Nellie, what are you doing here?!" I drop all my stuff on the floor when I see her lurking in my house.

"I wanted to talk."

"You know there is something called ringing the doorbell and not breaking into someone's house!!" I replied angrily.

I have never had someone follow me into my own home. I didn't know whether to go along with it or just call the police, to be honest. She lives right across the street from me, but I have never seen her this close to my house before. We were going to invite them to dinner, but it was around that time that Nellie still hated my guts.

She seems to have come around now, literally and figuratively.

"I passed out in math class." She hit me with the truth relatively quickly.

"Were you hydrated?" I have passed out many times while playing football, but those were in my early years when I was too stubborn to listen to the coach and stay hydrated.

"I got a 99 on my test." I didn't see the reason to pass out over an extremely high A in the most difficult class our school offers. I am so confused about what is happening right now. I am talking to a girl that didn't like me a few hours ago and she is now in my house talking about her problems like I'm her therapist.

She follows me when I pick up my bags and head to my room. I look back every once and a while to see if she has left yet. She is not in a good place right now, so it would be rude of me to kick her out of my house.

"So, this is your bedroom?" She looks around to see my five football trophies sitting on my dresser when you walk in, all below a massive poster highlighting my favorite player, Josh Allen. He plays for the Buffalo Bills and I think he looks like an older version of me. I have no reason to like him other than the fact that my dad has always liked him and that is the only thing we have bonded over.

I place my stuff down on my bed and let her know I need to use the restroom. I hope that she doesn't do anything or touch anything, I don't like the idea of her being in my house in the first place. I may like her a lot, but I would prefer for her to come over formally. Right now, it just feels like I am holding a refugee.

I run into the restroom quickly to prevent anything from happening and I never know when my parents are randomly going to show up out of the blue to check on me. Yet, I doubt that will ever happen shortly.

I slam the door shut and keep it unlocked in case of an emergency because you never really know what will happen. I eventually return to my bedroom and I see that she has found a spot on my bed, meaning she is asleep on my bed.

If my parents saw this right now, they would flip our whole house over. That is the only rule they have given me, keep girls out of the house and especially off of your bed. I try to figure out how I am going to politely tell her to get out and go home.

"Nellie, are you okay?" She opens her eyes to see that I have entered my bedroom again.

"I'm okay. Can we just talk about something other than school right now?" I try so hard not to tell her that if I told her to get out then it wouldn't be talking about school because then we wouldn't have to talk at all and we can live happily ever after as a normal couple, uhh friends. I sit down on the bed next to her instead and try to listen to what she wants to say.

"Jacoby, I was wrong about you. I..." There was suddenly a crazy loud bang on the front door cutting off

Nellie from finishing what she was saying. We both look in the direction of the noise.

"Mr. and Mrs. Briant, are you home? This is Mrs. Peterson, we were wondering if you have seen Nellie!!" We both notice that it is Nellie's mother at the door. She sounds panicked and on the verge of tears. I don't know why she is at my door, I guess she is just knocking on all of the neighbors' doors until someone responds with a "yes".

Nellie hides under my blankets and I try to convince her to go to her mom at the house. But, she refuses to and instead buries herself deeper into my bed. I hate that she is under my silk blankets with her wet body after the rain hit her pretty hard. She is really making me rethink this whole "liking her thing".

She breaks into my house and then doesn't want to leave when her mom is asking for her. I guess she is in enough trouble as it is with the super low 99 she got on her math test. I don't understand what happened to her parents when they were younger, I guess they didn't learn from failure because they just "never failed." That seems strange in my opinion.

I get up to get the door and Nellie reaches her hand towards me to pull me down again. I rip her hand off of me and I walk out of the room. I would enjoy her company a lot more if she wasn't so stressed about grades. Now I would have to encounter the mother for the first time in an improper fashion. This family just doesn't know proper hospitality I guess. At least her mother didn't break in too.

I grab the door and turn it, then I almost fall flat on my behind when her mom comes rushing in. No "hello", no "how are you doing, a person I never met?" I feel like I should report both of their behavior to the authorities, but I'm more scared of them than the authorities.

"What did you do with her?!" She just assumes I did something to her child that ran away from their house. I don't think I did anything. I love how the first time I meet her parents, I am already in trouble with something.

I shouldn't have even let her past the foyer, but I am a gentleman enough to show her mother to my bedroom where Nellie is badly hiding under a few silk sheets.

Her mother hits me upside the head causing me to have to massage that area.

"Mrs. Peterson, your daughter broke into our house!" I informed her in a polite, but stern manner.

"Was she let in?" I guess she was let in, but that is not my point. She didn't break through a window or knock down one of our doors, but I still don't appreciate that she came when she was not invited.

"Petranella Peterson, up now and to your bedroom!" I finally sighed in relief because they would be leaving.

Her mother picked her up and threw the blankets she was hiding under onto my pillows. I watched them like a hawk as they left to make sure they didn't commit any more crimes in my presence.

I hear the front door slam shut. Their voices fade away and I can now breathe.

I never thought that a fish could reel itself in.

Gone

The next morning during Biology class, I look around the room for Nellie. She is nowhere to be found. She might just be sick, so I don't think about it much longer.

She has been through a whole lot in the course of a few hours, so I wouldn't blame her. It feels weird not talking to her in the morning and we also have to finish our project by the end of the week. And I think she is well aware that I cannot complete that task on my own.

But, her parents do seem to care more about her school education than her health, so I don't know if she would miss school. But, if she was sick, her educational experience wouldn't be ideal for her to absorb any information.

"Are you looking for Nells?" I feel a tap on my shoulder and I look to find Dana standing right behind me.

"Well, she's not here for you to bully her. So give it up." Dana has never been the sweetest to me and today I think she forgot to drink her coffee because her left eye is twitching aggressively. She must not know about our current relationship or the fact that Nellie wanted to talk to me so much that she legitimately broke into my house to do so. If that is not love, I don't know what is. Dana seems to still think that I just always wanted to pick on her.

"Where is she, Dana?" I am concerned about Nellie and I hope that Dana can hear that concern in my tone. But, at the same time, I have not made the best reputation for myself and I guess that is just my fault.

"I'll tell you at lunch." Dana and I share lunch, but I am so confused as to why this conversation can't just happen now in Biology class. I don't think being sick is something to be ashamed of, but maybe she has some type of nasty disease.

I raised my hand to tell Mrs. Berkeley and she just thought I should work alone for the day. Mrs. Berkeley must not even know what happened to Nellie.

I pull out my notebook and continue to write down what comes to my mind about Carbohydrates. My mind wanders back to Nellie somehow and I get lost drawing her instead of the Carbohydrate structure. I shade her blue eyes with a bright blue highlighter and fill in her modest lips with a dark pink colored pencil I find on the floor next to my desk.

"Nice nerd Nellie portrait dude!" I glare over at Johnny to find him whispering into another boy's ear. My face starts to grow hotter and I feel like I could fry an egg on my forehead at this point. I curl up my fingers and form a fist on both of my hands.

I walk over to Liam and signal him to move to the right a tad. He follows my instruction and I move in closer to Johnny, practically touching noses with him.

Mrs. Berkeley left the classroom to refill her water bottle a few minutes ago and if she didn't, she would probably be telling me to sit down right now. But, I'm not going to sit down until I am respected.

This is a free country and I should be allowed to have a relationship with whoever I want. A dude that eats pickles out of a plastic bag every morning should not have the right to manage my life.

"Did you want to tell me something?" I am trying to hold back so much anger and it is difficult for me to not just sucker punch him right now. I want to handle this responsibly because his dad determines my future ultimately if I continue to get better at football.

"Your girlfriend is u-g-l-y." He says with the biggest smile on his face. I breathe in and out, thinking of my future on the football team. Then I remember, Nellie is my future, not a sports team filled with judgemental people that act like they are my friends.

Nellie may have broken into my house, but at least she cares about me and will break the law to talk to me. Not one person on my football team would do that for me if I told them to.

He backs up to sit back down in his seat, but I wrap my hands around the back of his head. He puts his hands up and grips my arms, but I Up Knee him. My knee knocks straight into his face at this point and blood is dripping out of his nose.

He smears the blood around his face in hopes of wiping it away. His face is covered in blood now and some students start surrounding both of us, holding their iPhones up at our faces.

He backs up again and falls onto his desk. His knees lay straight out and I stomp on one of them, causing it to make a loud popping sound.

His tears start to mix with the blood covering his face and he falls onto the floor holding onto the knee I just stomped on. All reality suddenly hits me and I look around to see students laughing and talking amongst one another. I am in awe of what I have just done. Why did I just do this?

"Jacoby Briant!" And of course, Mrs. Berkeley returns to the classroom right when the commotion hits its peak. I look into her eyes and my heart starts to beat out of my chest. I don't recall doing any of this, I look down at Johnny's face then back up at Mrs. Berkeley.

"Uh." Is the only word I can utter, or it sounds more like a sound. I start to fast forward into the future in my brain.

My parents are probably never going to let me out of their sight again or put up dozens of cameras or take away my car forever. I can't imagine what punishment I am going to get from the school.

Mrs. Berkeley runs over to her phone and types in three digits, most likely the number to get an ambulance to come to the school. For the next few minutes, she disregards looking at Johnny at all. I don't know how that would possibly help him. I try to hold back tears as they are about to erupt out of every hole in my face.

"Jacoby, up to the principal's office. Your parents will meet you there." She doesn't even look in my direction, and I have to interpret every other word. Her face is also bright red and she continues to stroke her eyes, likely keeping them dry.

I predicted that I would have to go up to Principal Keenan. He is tough and has always loved me because he is very much into all sports. He even attends all of the football games.

I'm guessing he is not going to be too thrilled to hear that I just got into a fight with the coach's son, even though I should have done this a long time ago. Johnny is not just mean to me, he always makes fun of every other guy on the team, but we are all too scared to mention it to the coach for the sake of our positions on the team.

Johnny doesn't even play football, he just sits on the bench and sometimes is the waterboy when his dad makes him do something slightly productive with his time. I feel as though I did this for the rest of the team, but I doubt that Principal Keenan is going to take that as an excuse. We have cameras in every classroom in the school, but I didn't think that far ahead until I finished fighting. They have direct evidence pointing all the blame to me because the school was too cheap to buy cameras with microphones attached, proving that Johnny has always bullied me in class.

Again, if I say anything, it just ends up leading to more harm than good.

I make it to the top of the fourth floor where the principal's office is. It is down the hallway, so with every step, it gradually gets harder to walk any further.

I hate long hallways, especially when there is someone you are going to meet and they are standing there staring at you.

Principal Keenan steps out of his office to greet me with a slow wave of his hand. He doesn't look mad, so I am hopeful. But, at the same time, he rarely actually looks legitimately mad.

"JB, what's up?!" Okay, so I guess he is in a good mood today. I know he likes me, but I pretty much just knocked out a kid in my class for talking badly about a girl that I barely know.

I walk into his office to be greeted by both of my parents. They look delighted to be here, they must have not heard the news or I am in an alternate universe.

"Why don't you take a seat, Jacoby."

I listen and take a seat right in between both of my parents. It is so weird that the environment is not as tense as I envisioned it would be. I don't know what is going on here, but I do know somebody better fill me in or I might explode.

"Jacoby, you're off the football team and suspended for two weeks." My mouth falls open and I am in great shock. The environment starts to get tense and I stand up out of my seat. My parents still have that annoying delighted look on their faces.

"What?! Are you guys happy about this?" I finally erupt.

"We thought it was time for you to get some work done in the house and also we feel like football is not good for your mental health. It is making you quite destructive." My mom implies.

"Football is the only thing keeping me together. I finally had someone at school that cares about me, now I am not going to be able to talk to her and you both are happy about that?!"

They both shrug their shoulders like they didn't just hear a single word that came out of my mouth. They have spent so much time in that awful bakery, that they don't even know how to raise their child anymore.

Away from Him

I usually trust my parents' judgment. But, these last few days, I have questioned their decisions.

They pulled me out of my old school where I was able to go to school with Dana and Jacoby, now I am in a new school filled with people I don't even know.

I am so incredibly angry at life right now, I am taken away from my whole life that I had worked so hard to survive before, and now because of a 99 on an AP Calculus test, I am living a completely new life. And there is nothing I can do because I am only 15 years old, so I can't move out of my parent's house.

They think that Jacoby was a bad influence on me and is only bringing my grade down. I had to tell them about everything because they can tell when I am lying, it is fairly easy to tell and I can't help that every time I lie, my hands start to shake. I guess I could have told them half of the truth, but I wouldn't be able to live with myself.

"Petranella Peterson, did I say that correctly?" I hear a lot of chuckles behind me as my new PE teacher, Mr. Watts tries to call the roll.

"Yeah, that's right." I now have PE first and I hate it, I have to get up and play a sport in this school. There is a "no sitting" policy and it makes that first ten minutes terrible. I heard that as soon as I walked into the gymnasium and I automatically knew that I wasn't going to like this new school.

"Okay, everyone warm up with your teams then break off for play." I hardly understand any of the words coming out of his mouth because I usually just hand back on the bleachers and ignore any form of authority in the gym. I usually like to take advantage of the time to do anything other than physical activity.

But from the looks of things, it seems like they take the "no sitting" policy seriously.

I stand up from my bottom seat on the bleachers and start walking in the direction of other girls in my section of the gym. In my peripheral vision, I see my assigned coach pointing at me and mouthing the word, "you".

I turn towards him and stand a considerable distance away from him since we just met and I'm not fond of talking to strangers anyway. They may have been background checked, but you never know with men who have scruffy black beards, who sound like they have been smoking for hundreds of years and they're your gym coach.

"Hey, I heard what happened to get you here. Was it a 99 that ticked your folks off?" He seemed very intrigued with my story and I didn't feel comfortable opening up to him on day one, but I didn't think I had a choice.

"Yeah." He started to rub his beard and his mouth opened extremely wide. It was like he had never heard a story like that before.

"Usually, people come to this school because they've punched a kid, not because they're doing great in school."

I nodded my head in agreement with his overall opinions and I was interested in his character, none of my teachers have shown this much interest in me at all.

"When I was a kid, life was rough, but my folks let me be a kid. Not to assume your parent's vibe, but I think they need you to be a kid. Grades are just some numbers that some old guy probably came up with." He looked down at me waiting for a response, but I just looked around the gym to avoid making eye contact with him again.

"You're not much of a chatter, are you?" I shake my head and he walks over to the bleachers. I follow him because the students are doing lunges and I can barely sit down sometimes without my knees popping.

I sit a few feet away from him and he scrunches his face up while looking at me. I slid in a little closer and he signaled me to come in closer. I don't know about him, but I am not a fan of smelling what other people ate for breakfast.

"What do you know?" He asked me.

I shrug my shoulders and he tilts his face to the side, he even makes my signature duck face. I giggle and then look up at the ceiling briefly. I don't know whether he wants me to start spewing out facts or tell him what I recently learned.

"I know about Calculus, Algebra, Biology.."

"Okay, now what have you learned?" I was so confused. I thought he just asked that question a few seconds ago. I close my mouth and then think. What have I learned? This shouldn't be too hard for me to come up with, I study like crazy for every test.

"I can't recall anything at the moment, sorry." He looks at me to hear that response then looks at the crowd in the gym. I look at the students too.

"You care so much about your grades, that you forgot about the most important part of school." He had hand gestures for every word to help me understand.

"What do you mean?" I question his advice since, after all, he is just a gym teacher. I am not going to take advice from someone who probably doesn't even remember math.

"When was the last time you just learned to learn?" I thought for a moment. I honestly cannot even come up with a fake answer to that question.

Everything I have done in school, I have just done for the perfect score in the gradebook. I don't remember the last time I enjoyed school. I enjoy the 100s in the grade book, but that is only to please my unforgiving parents.

"That's what I thought." I hate that statement. He is saying that he knows more than me, which I will never allow to be true. If he knew more than me, he would be a surgeon or a lawyer, or even a real teacher.

"Nice meeting you, it was cool to talk to you, Petronella was it?" I extend my hand to shake his hand just to be polite. His hand's grip is intense and a little moist.

"You can call me Nellie. No one calls me Petronella anymore." I can tell that he takes that into account with the nod of his head.

"Whether you like it or not, I think it is a beautiful name." I can't help but smile at his unexpected comment, but I try to pull it back so he doesn't think I like him.

Later that night, I decided to open the forbidden room with a hairpin I find under my mattress. My parents are both asleep and they don't know I am awake.

I can even hear my dad snoring through their bedroom door. I know they are both asleep because their radio is no longer on and they have turned off their lights.

I find my phone tucked in one of my dresser drawers. I pull it out and turn it on using the button on the side of it. I run back into my bedroom and plop down on my bed.

I look for the keypad app on my home screen. Once I locate it, I tap on it to open it up. I hold my head upright because I am so incredibly tired, but I refuse to go to sleep until I see Jacoby again. It has been too long and I need to see someone that cares about me for a change.

I type in a few digits, hoping that I recalled it correctly, then press the call button. Jacoby has always had his phone number plastered on his school bag in case it ever got stolen and I have been trained to memorize numbers in certain orders. I never thought it would come in handy for something I care about.

I look down and see that it is calling someone and they haven't hung up yet, so there is still hope. I don't have an alternative plan if it doesn't work. But, I am just hoping that it works. Suddenly the phone stops ringing and there is just a moment of complete silence.

"Hello, who is this?" I hear from the other end of the line. I can't tell if it is Jacoby or not because of the awful microphone quality, so I give the individual as little information as possible so they don't track me to my house.

"Hey, Nellie! What's up! It is so good to hear your voice." I blush a little bit then my mind goes blank. I don't even know why I called him in the first place, it is nice to hear his voice as well. Our relationship has barely started and it already feels like everyone is trying to break it up. Because of a single stupid grade, I am not allowed to see the guy I love... I mean the guy I like.

"Want to walk to the library?" I came up with it at the very last second.

The other end goes dead silent again. Then I look back at my phone to see that he hung up completely.

I throw my phone across my room and then pull my blankets over my head. I curl up in a small ball and start to cry.

I can't do anything else, I am not in control of my life anymore, I have never been in control of my life. The coach may have been right, I've never had the chance to just be a kid. My parents find value in my grades, not me.

I hear a knock at my window and I peek at the window. It is Jacoby.

"You really want to go?" He yells through the window. I nod my head and jump out of my bed to walk towards my window.

"Nellie, are you okay?!" I hear my mother's voice coming from right outside of my bedroom. I sprint to close the window blinds when I hear her gasp enter the room.

"Is that Jacoby, again?!" It is the scariest sounding voice I have ever heard. She sounds like she might actually implode if she takes another step.

I look back out the window and Jacoby is running back to his house.

She turns on my lights and stomps over in my direction. She grabs my arm and drags me to their bedroom across the hallway. By turning on her light as well, my dad wakes up as well and he doesn't like to be woken up in the middle of the light.

"Are you stupid?" She questions. I look at my dad to see how he reacts to her blunt question. He looks frustrated at my mom, but then has the same face when turning to look at me.

"No.. I don't think I am." I try to answer in a mature tone, tears are building up, but I hold them back.

"Yes, you are. There is no value in you and you are stupid. All you had to do was just get a 100. How hard is that?" She is roaring now and my dad is now looking back at her, he looks worried when he looks in my direction.

"I hate you!" It just spills out of my mouth and I cover my mouth quickly in surprise.

"Go to your room now! And if I see that child again with you, I am calling the police! Do you hear me, Petronella?!"

I stomp into my room, completely ignoring all of the following words that come out of her mouth. I hate the person that created grades so much! I have missed out on life because this person decided to rank each individual in every school based on a number.

Surprises

Dana is my only friend left because Nellie's parents shut me off from even coming near Nellie. Dana has come around with me ever since I admitted to her that I liked Nellie.

Last night at Nellie's house when I had to run for my life, I went back to my house to text Dana about what to do to get in touch with Nellie. Dana is pretty smart when it comes to surprising people, so we both crafted a plan to surprise Nellie at school this morning.

Since I'm not in football anymore, my mornings have looked a lot different and I have a lot of free time to kill. Dana suggested that we write her a card and bring some candy to her school to surprise her.

Dana's parents agreed to take both of us to the school. I was suspended from my school, not Nellie's, so technically they couldn't charge me for trespassing.

I heard the doorbell ring and I went to the door to see who it was. I assumed it was just Dana and I was correct.
"Hey, how are you doing? No football now, right?"

"Yeah, that's what you get for beating up a kid who had it coming for him I guess."

She laughs and I show her to the kitchen table where I have the card and the jar of candy.

"You can sign it if you want."

She walks over to the card and picks up a pen that is sitting on the table next to the card. She signs the card quickly and picks it up with the jar of candy. I follow her out the door and down to her mom's gray jeep.

She honks her horn to greet me and it is enlightening if I account for all the things that have happened to me over the past week.

Both Dana and I sit in the seats in the back of the car. I take the ask for the card from Dana so I can read it over again and Dana holds on to the jar of candy. The card reads:

Hey Nellie!

Dana and I both care deeply about you and know you are going through a pretty tough time right now, to say the least. I know that times may get tough like this, but I would like to let you know that you will always have our shoulders to cry on and our time if you ever want to talk about anything. I know this candy won't help much to solve any of the problems going on, but I hope it reminds you that we love you!

See you soon,
Jacoby and Dana

Dana read the letter over my shoulder and hugged me. It was my very first hug from her ever. It is crazy how things have changed.

I hope that Nellie isn't hating her new school that much and that she is making some new friends, not too close though. I still do have a crush on her after all.

"Aren't you both such nice friends? I guess I did something right when I was raising you, sweet Dawny bug." I could see Dana's mother's face from inside the rearview mirror and it looked like her eyes were red.

I didn't think that she would honestly ever let us do this, but I guess she could see our hearts behind it when Dana explained it to her in the morning.

My parents don't even know that I'm doing this right now. I just have to stay home now and they are always at the bakery, so they would never know when I left the house.

We finally arrive at Nellie's school after a few miles down the road. It is relatively closer than our other school, almost making me wonder why we didn't just go there instead. I hand Dana back the card after I seal it in a blue envelope. I just figured that blue was her favorite color since almost all of her school supplies were blue.

Nellie's mom pulls around to the front of the school while both Dana and I walk to the big array of doors.

I ring the doorbell since Dana is holding the gifts.

"Who are you and what are you here for?" It sounds like the front office lady that I can see through the glass doors on a phone, but her voice sounds super crackly.

"Our names are Dana and Jacoby, we are just here to drop off a gift for our friend that goes to this school." Dana says in an extremely sweet tone.

There is a long pause, but then the light on the door turns green so we can open the door to come in. I held the door open for Dana and she slid in to greet the lady she was talking to. I followed quickly behind her.

"What's the student's name and grade?" She asked.

"Nellie.. sorry, I meant Petronella Peterson and she is a freshman." I informed her.

She started typing loudly on her desktop computer. It seemed like it was a computer from ancient times. I guess Nellie's school was built a while ago or their budget just goes towards other things.

She looks up at both of us confused.

"It says here on the attendance logged-in, that Petronella isn't here. Sorry, I don't know what to tell you."

Dana looks at me and I turn to look over at her. I am flustered, it is like absolutely nothing can go the way I intended.

I caught the fish on my hook, she got on my boat then flopped back off into the ocean.

"I guess we have to go, Jacoby." Dana just gives up, I don't know why Nellie wouldn't show up to school. I mean there are lots of reasons for the average student not to show up, but how is she supposed to get a 100 in her classes if she is not in her classes? Something seemed strange.

"We have to go to her house." Dana looks at me like I am a chicken running around without a head.

"Are you crazy?! At this point, her parents could call the authorities on you." Dana's voice gets increasingly shaky and I put my arm over her. I am confident that there is nothing else worse that can go wrong, so I am not afraid to take a shot to get back to Nellie.

We both turn around and walk down the stairs to meet Dana's mom in her car.

"What happened?" She questioned while looking at Dana's face then the card and candy still sitting in her hands.

We tell her that Nellie is not at the school and we need to find her. We suspect she just stayed home for the day, but nobody could predict where she wants to be right now.

The Gradebook

Water is so beautiful and so lucky. It doesn't have to worry about parents or grades in the grade book. It has no classes to go to and no people it has to talk to. I wonder what would happen if I gave the water all of my life. All of my problems, it wouldn't know how to handle them and likely spit me back out.

I would spit myself out, to be honest. I peer over the edge of the bridge. There is just water for miles. I take off my jacket and I take off my watch.

I hope the water doesn't spit me out because I want to think like the ocean. I don't want to have to worry about my grades anymore or my parents who care about my grades or my classes who hand out grades.

I close my eyes.

I smell the salt lifted off of the water's surface.

I feel the gentle breeze of the tide coming in.

I hear the cheerful baby birds talking to their friends.

I taste the cold wet air on my tongue when I open my mouth.

I open my eyes and see the sea, just the sea, and the straight horizon line, separating the water from the large light blue sky.

There is no sound of people. No sound of bustling cars. No sound of a school bell. No sound of a red Sharpie marker squeaking as it writes on your paper.

It is just nature. No worries at all, I sense it all around me. It is beautiful. Every child was away at school and every adult was away at work. It was just me and myself. It has been 15 years since that has occurred.

I hold onto the edge of the wooden beams holding up the bridge. I take a deep breath and plant my feet on the first cross-section on the bridge.

I close my eyes and breathe again. This time I am a lot higher off the ground.

This time I hear a great vibration coming from the front of the bridge, but I ignore it as it is not of this peaceful nature I am sitting in.

I hear panting behind me, from a human. I hope that it is just a tourist and they don't communicate with me.

"Nellie!" Oh no, they know my name. I have to speed this process up, so I never hear the words coming from a human's mouth again. These past few days have only been a nightmare and I don't want to ever relive it.

"I love you. I know that may sound weird coming from your teacher. But, I love you and I would really like to see you in my class tomorrow. I know I'm just a PE teacher, but I really really care about you Nellie." Tears start to rush down my face. Why would he care about me, he's only known me for an hour. Why would he love me, I'm not perfect and my parents have made that abundantly clear.

"Don't do this, Nellie or I will jump in with you and pull you out." I turn around and Jacoby is standing next to Coach Watts. They are both crying and I don't know what I did to make them cry.

I jump down from off the ledge and give them both a hug. They squeeze so tight that they nearly suck all of the air out of me.

I look over to see my whole school at the front of the bridge looking at me. Why are they all here, I wonder. I don't even know any of them. Except for Dana who is in front of the piled-up group.

"They heard your story and they knew what you were thinking of doing and where you were thinking of going." Coach Watts looks into my eyes with such joy on his face, like he found what he has been looking for for years now.

I look around and don't see my parents anywhere in sight. I hug Jacoby again just to make sure I am still here and he is still real.

I hear a familiar voice in the distance. Not one I want to hear though.

"Let go of my child, Jacoby. We have the police ready to arrest you." My mother is pointing three policemen in the direction of Jacoby and Coach Watts.

Coach Watts signals me to get behind him and back up. He walks over to my mother and stands in front of her face.

"Nellie is a 15-year-old girl, a child, your child. She should not be ranked or valued based on a number in her grade book. You know the real grade book, the one that speaks to her kindness, compassion, and generosity. And you want her to have a 100, she already does and she always did." Coach Watts looks back at me on the verge of tears again.

I ran up to hug him.

I look over at the policeman holding the handcuffs.

"Sir, if you look behind you. All of these people know what my mother and father have done to me for the past years. If you don't believe me or Coach Watts, believe them. They are my 100 other witnesses. The person you should be arresting is the lady that sent you down here" I look up into the officer's eyes.

"Is this true?" The officer looks back at the crowd. They all nod their heads and he handcuffs my mom.

"Mam, we are not going to take you in, but we are going to get you and your husband some serious help.

Nellie, was it?" I nod my head in response to his question.

"I think you might have a pretty good teacher to look after you while your parents are gone." I look back at Mr. Watts and he looks at the officer to nod his head.

I give my mom a small hug and two kisses on her cheek.

"That second one is for Dad. Don't lose it. I love you!" I watch as she walks away and crouches down to sit in the police car, we all wave as she drives away.

I now turn over to Jacoby.

"Do you like me, Jacoby?"

"Yes, Petronella. And I only want to be with you more because you are yourself."

Author's Note

I come from a family led by both an amazing, determined, loving mother and father. Nellie's, Jacoby's, and Dana's parents are no different. This book is not meant to highlight any sort of parenting style as being the absolute best one. The individuals we are raised by come in all shapes, colors, backgrounds, and numbers. This novel was not directly inspired by my life but by my experience surrounded by so many young voices. Grades ranking a child's value should not even be a thing. I believe they are meant to mark growth, not for comparison amongst other students. A child should not strive for a certain number, but I believe they should strive for mastery and confidence. Thanks to my lovely teachers I have had and parents that taught me to try my hardest, I am writing this novel for all the students that are not allowed to just learn to learn. Thank you!

Made in the USA
Columbia, SC
06 May 2023

f46da103-f887-4a05-8f88-1c2c0b6be2c5R01